Thank You Earth
Our Beautiful Home

by Jennifer Waddell

Printed in Canada by Friesens Corporation
ISBN 978-0-692-86432-6

Thank You Earth Our Beautiful Home
Illustrations and text by Jennifer Waddell
Production design by Marcia Moore

For my mom, Kathleen.

Thank you for your unwavering love and support.

I love you this much!

Can you find
the heart on
each page?

Thank you, sun,
for bringing the day.

Thank you, moon,
for lighting my way.

Thank you, rain,
for the water you bring.

Thank you, birds,
for the song you sing.

Thank you, trees,
for your fruit,
and your shade.

Thank you, bees,
for the honey you made.

Thank you, fire,
for your warmth,
and your light.

Thank you, flowers,
for your colors so bright.

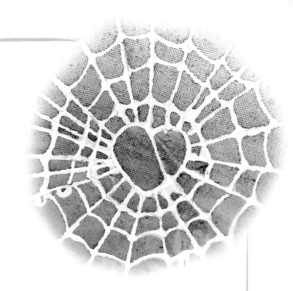

Thank you, spider,
for the webs you weave.

Thank you, plants,
for the oxygen we breathe.

Thank you, ocean,
for your beauty and grace.

Thank you, wind,
for cooling my face.

Thank you, family,
for helping me grow.

Thank you, friend,
for loving me so.

Thank you, great spirit,
for I am never alone.

Thank you, earth,
our beautiful home!

Jennifer lives in Santa Cruz, California with her two awesome children and their sweet bunny rabbit, Koa. She enjoys painting, hanging out with her kids, running in the forest, singing and cooking. This is her first children's book.